Monsters

by Lucille Recht Penner
illustrated by Allen Douglas

A STEPPING STONE BOOK™
Random House New York

To Ben —L.R.P.

To my own little monsters, Ava and Ella
—A.D.

Text copyright © 2009 by Lucille Recht Penner
Illustrations copyright © 2009 by Allen Douglas

Visit us on the Web!
www.steppingstonesbooks.com
www.randomhouse.com/kids

Educators and librarians, for a variety of teaching tools, visit us at
www.randomhouse.com/teachers

Library of Congress Cataloging-in-Publication Data
Penner, Lucille Recht.
Monsters / by Lucille Recht Penner ; illustrated by Allen Douglas. — 1st ed.
  p.   cm.
"A stepping stone book."
ISBN 978-0-375-85675-4 (pbk.) — ISBN 978-0-375-95675-1 (lib. bdg.)
1. Monsters—Juvenile literature. I. Douglas, Allen, ill. II. Title.
GR825.P43 2009   398.24'54—dc22   2008048588

Printed in the United States of America

10 9 8 7 6 5 4 3 2 1

Contents

1 Here Be Monsters   1

2 Monsters on Land   7

3 Monsters at Sea   18

4 Flying Monsters   27

5 Monsters or Men?   37

1

HERE BE MONSTERS

It's midnight in the forest. Suddenly a streak of lightning slashes across the sky. Thunder crashes overhead. Glowing eyes stare out of the darkness. Then heavy footsteps shake the ground. What is coming? Could it be a monster?

Long ago, people believed in monsters. They thought there were monsters on land, in the sea, and in the sky. What else could cause so many scary things?

Today we know what causes volcanoes and earthquakes. But back then, nobody knew. People thought earthquakes must be caused by fighting giants. They thought

volcanoes came from dragons breathing fire.

Early sailors didn't understand storms. Sometimes a big wave flipped over a boat. Sailors thought an angry sea monster had done it.

The sky might turn as dark as night in the middle of the day. It was an eclipse. The moon had passed between the sun and the earth. But people didn't know that. They thought a huge bird had blotted out the sun.

No one actually saw a monster. But people felt they had proof. They pointed to the giant bones of birds that had weighed half a ton. They had no idea the birds were much too heavy to fly. And they didn't know the birds had died out long ago.

Once in a while, an enormous tentacle washed up on a beach. It was part of a giant squid. Giant squids can weigh 2,000

pounds. Most of the time, they stay deep underwater. But anyone who saw parts of them easily believed they were monsters.

And what about huge skulls with one hole in the middle of the forehead? They must have come from gigantic one-eyed monsters. Today we know that these are really the skulls of ancient elephants. The hole is where the elephant's trunk was attached.

But for a long time, nobody understood these things. People were sure they had just one meaning—scary monsters were everywhere!

2
MONSTERS ON LAND

"I'll eat you all!"

A cyclops was stamping around his dark cave. He was fifty feet tall. In the middle of his forehead was one eye. Men ran from him screaming. The cyclops grabbed a man and swallowed him headfirst. Then another man, and another. Finally the cyclops lay down across the opening of his cave.

"I'll eat the rest of you in the morning," he said. Then he closed his enormous eye and fell asleep.

Odysseus was the leader of a group of Greek soldiers. They had wandered into the cyclops's cave by mistake.

Odysseus made a plan to save his men. He took a burned stick from the fire. Quickly he stabbed it into the monster's eye to blind him.

But how could the men get out with the cyclops guarding the exit? The monster had a flock of sheep in his cave. Odysseus told his men to tie themselves to the sheeps' bellies.

In the morning, the cyclops let the sheep out to graze. He petted each one as it passed by him. He wanted to make sure only sheep left the cave—not Odysseus's men. But he didn't feel the men under the sheep. They escaped from the cave and ran away.

A cyclops was a type of giant that lived in Greece. Many were blacksmiths. The one Odysseus met herded sheep.

Greece seemed to be full of monsters. Medusa was the ugliest one. She was so ugly that anyone who saw her turned to stone. She had a huge black tongue and sharp fangs. And the worst part was what grew on her head. She had live snakes instead of hair!

Someone needed to get rid of Medusa. A Greek hero named Perseus decided he would do it. The gods helped him with two

amazing gifts. One was a magic helmet.
The other was a pair of winged sandals.

*Perseus put on the helmet. It made
him invisible. Then he put on the winged
sandals. Now he could fly!*

*He flew to Medusa's cave. There he found
the monster asleep. The cave was crowded
with statues of men. All of them had looked
at Medusa and been turned to stone.*

*Perseus was very careful not to look at
her. He looked only at her reflection in his
shiny shield. He sneaked up on her. Then,
with one terrific blow, he cut off her head!*

*Later, Perseus put Medusa's head on his
shield. It turned his enemies to stone!*

Another monster also had the "look of death." If you set eyes on a basilisk, you would fall down dead! There was only one way to save yourself. You had to hold a mirror in front of it. If a basilisk saw itself, it died of fright.

What did this monster look like? Nobody who saw one lived long enough to say. But

artists drew pictures of how they *thought* a basilisk looked. These pictures showed a monster with a rooster's head and legs and a snake's fangs and tail. It had wings covered with scales or feathers.

A basilisk could shatter rocks just by breathing on them. In one story, a man on horseback stabbed a basilisk with a long spear. He didn't look at it or touch it. But the monster's poisonous breath *rose up through the spear.* It killed the man—and his horse, too.

Many monsters used poison, including manticores. They lived in the jungles of Asia. "Manticore" means "eater of people."

What do you think was a manticore's favorite food?

A manticore had the body of a bright red lion and a scorpion's tail. But its face was human. It had blue eyes and a huge mouth with three rows of sharp teeth.

When it saw a person, it fired poisonous

spikes from the tip of its tail. The person fell over and the manticore gobbled up every bit of him—even his teeth, clothes, and shoes!

There were many manticores, but only one Minotaur. This monster had the body of a man and the head and tail of a bull. It lived in a large maze under the island of Crete.

Every year, Minos, the king of Crete, lowered seven boys and seven girls into the maze. The Minotaur hunted and ate them.

After many years, a Greek hero named Theseus came to kill the Minotaur. King Minos's daughter, Ariadne, fell in love with Theseus. She gave him a ball of thread and a sword.

Theseus tied one end of the thread at the maze's opening. He unwound the thread as he moved through the maze.

Finally he came upon the Minotaur. After a fierce battle, Theseus killed it with the sword. Then he followed the thread out of the maze. He sailed back to Greece with Ariadne.

Everyone knew where the Minotaur lived. But no one knew where other monsters were hiding. When people saw strange shapes far away or heard a hiss in the grass, they shivered with fear.

Was it a monster?

Was it coming for *them*?

3
MONSTERS AT SEA

What lives far beneath the waves? No one really knows. Huge monsters could be hidden there, deep down in the dark.

Long ago, sailors were afraid of sea monsters. When rough waves tossed their boats, they thought monsters were trying to shake them into the sea. At any moment, one might rise up and pull them under.

Mapmakers wrote a warning across the oceans—"Here Be Monsters." Sailor, beware!

Imagine fishing on top of a monster! Some Norwegian fishermen took that risk. The fish they wanted swarmed around a sea monster called a kraken. This creature was the size of a small island. It was one and a half miles wide!

Usually a kraken floated peacefully in the sea. But if it dived, it made a huge whirlpool. Fish, sailors, and ships were all sucked deep into the water.

Krakens had big, staring eyes and sharp horns. They could wrap their long arms around a ship and pull it under. Sometimes they pulled down whole fishing fleets and ate them!

Other water monsters lived in the lakes and swamps of Australia. They were called bunyips. Bunyips were dark, hairy creatures. They had long tails, sharp tusks, and big claws. If a child fell into a lake or swamp, bunyips gobbled him up. When

children heard the cry of a bunyip, they
turned and ran away from the water as fast
as they could.

A Japanese water monster, the kappa, also liked to eat children. But there was a trick that kids could play on a kappa. This monster couldn't live away from the water. So whenever it came out on land, it carried water with it in a little hollow on top of its head.

"Watch out!"

A boy was playing near the river when he heard a shout. His father was standing above him on a cliff and pointing. The boy turned around.

A kappa had jumped out of the river and was coming toward him. It was hideous! It looked like a monkey with a beak in the middle of its face. It had scaly

yellow skin and a hard shell on its back.

The boy started to run, but his father yelled, "Stop! Turn around and bow!"

The boy bowed to the monster. Even though kappas were fierce, they were also polite. When the boy bowed, the monster bowed back—and the water on top of its head spilled out. The monster gave a horrible cry and ran back to the river.

But what if you didn't know that trick? Suppose a kappa *did* grab you. It still might let you go if your parents gave it a gift.

Gold? Silver? Diamonds? No. The gift that worked best with a kappa was *cucumbers.*

If a family took a swim, they brought cucumbers with them. Each person wrote his name on a cucumber. They threw the cucumbers into the water before jumping in. That kept them safe from kappas.

Another water monster, the Midgard Serpent, was so long it could circle the whole world! This huge monster was the child of a Norse god and a giantess. As soon as it was born, the Midgard Serpent began to grow.

The king of the gods was sure the serpent was evil. He flung it far out into the ocean. Under the water, the serpent grew and grew. Finally it was so big, it wrapped itself around the world. It bit its tail to make a great circle.

Sea monsters seemed to live in every river, lake, and ocean. No wonder people were afraid near water. But the sky was just as dangerous. Flying monsters might be up there, ready to swoop down and grab them.

4
FLYING MONSTERS

ATTENTION!

THE SHOGUN IS COMING FOR A VISIT.

PLEASE LEAVE THIS MOUNTAINTOP

FOR THREE DAYS.

In 1860, Japanese soldiers left this sign high on a mountain. It wasn't for people. It was for tengus. Tengus were flying

monsters that lived in the mountains.

Tengus were also shape-changers. They could make themselves look like huge birds. Or they could look like people with red faces and long noses. When they looked human, tengus carried fans made of feathers. Every time they shook the fans, tornadoes roared down from the sky.

Tengus caused all kinds of trouble. Sometimes one would speak through a woman's mouth. It said weird things, so people thought she was crazy. Sometimes tengus challenged men to sword fights. That was scary. Nobody ever won a fight with a tengu.

The government of Japan didn't take any chances. When an important person came to the mountains for a visit, soldiers put up signs. They asked the tengus to please stay away.

Signs might work with tengus. But nothing worked with Harpies.

"Harpy" is a name that means "grabber." Harpies had mighty wings, ugly faces, and fierce claws. They had bodies like women's. And they had ears like a bear's. They lived on a Greek island, but they often flew over the water to gobble up sailors.

Harpies were filthy and smelly. No

matter how much they ate, they were
always hungry.

If Harpies saw someone eating food,
they grabbed for it. If they touched it even

for a second, it would smell horrible and taste awful. No human could eat it. But Harpies loved it that way.

The most famous flying monster is the roc. It looked like a huge vulture with big claws and sharp horns on its head.

How big were rocs? They were big enough to pick up elephants with their beaks! They carried the elephants high into the sky and dropped them. The elephants burst into pieces on the ground below. Then the rocs flew down to gobble them up.

Sinbad the Sailor was a brave man, but rocs terrified him. Sinbad was a hero in *The Arabian Nights,* a book written in

Arabic hundreds of years ago. He was
born in Iraq and sailed the world.

*Sinbad was stranded on an island. At
least it seemed to be an island. A white
dome took up most of it.*

*But the dome didn't have any doors or
windows. In fact, it wasn't a building at all.
It was a roc's egg. The island was really a
roc's nest!*

*Suddenly huge wings blocked the light of
the sun. The bright day turned into night.
The mother roc was coming! She didn't see
Sinbad as she settled onto her egg.*

*How could Sinbad escape? He had an
idea. He unwound his turban into a long*

strip of cloth. He used the cloth to tie
himself to one of the roc's feet.

The roc flew off with Sinbad hanging
beneath her! Finally she landed. Sinbad
untied the cloth and ran away.

Griffins weren't as big as rocs, but they
were just as dangerous. They had the bodies
of lions and the heads of eagles. They had
the tails of snakes and claws as sharp as
knives. Their eyes glowed red. Blue feathers
covered their heads and wings.

Griffins came from India, but they lived
in other countries, too. They liked shiny
things. They made their nests of gold.
Every day they flew out to find treasure.

They brought it back to their nests and guarded it carefully. If anyone came near, they tore him to pieces.

If you saw a bird monster coming, it was time to duck and run. But what should you do if you weren't sure just *what* was coming toward you—a man or a monster?

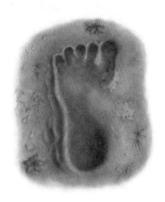

5
MONSTERS OR MEN?

In 1958, a crew was building a road in California. One morning, a worker found huge footprints nearby. A reporter wrote a story about the footprints. He called the creature that made them Bigfoot.

Almost ten years later, a rodeo cowboy named Roger Patterson made a film. It showed a Bigfoot running through the

woods. Most scientists thought the film showed a man wearing a gorilla costume.

Then a hunter snapped a photograph, using a camera tied to a tree. He said it was a picture of Bigfoot. Others said it was probably a sick bear.

One man even claimed to have *lived* with a group of Bigfeet. He was camping in the wilderness. One night, something picked him up, sleeping bag and all. It carried him a long way. Then it dumped him on the ground.

Four apemen stood over him. They seemed to be talking, but he didn't understand what they said. They didn't hurt him, and after a few days he was able to escape.

This was an interesting story. But there was no proof it was true. Many people claim to have seen a Bigfoot. Did they really? Was it a mistake? Or were they just playing a trick?

People described these monsters as half human and half ape. They said Bigfeet were covered with long, shaggy hair. Sometimes hair like that was found stuck on fences. Where did it come from?

Bigfeet walked on two legs, like humans. But they were much taller—eight, ten, even fifteen feet tall! And they smelled awful.

For some people, searching for Bigfoot is a hobby. They have formed Bigfoot clubs. They like to meet and share their Bigfoot stories. Some say they have heard a Bigfoot howling and screaming in the wilderness. One group of campers said a Bigfoot threw stones at them.

Bigfoot stories come from all around the world. In Nepal, people call these monsters yetis. When British explorers came to Nepal, they called them abominable snowmen. They believed they saw their

footprints in the snow. But some people think the footprints were made by Tibetan blue bears.

In China, an apeman called the Yeren is said to eat people. In Africa, people fear the Chemosit, an apeman that eats only people's *brains.* And Australians tell stories about the Yowie, a fierce apeman with red eyes and long fangs.

Some people think apemen are a "missing link" between monkeys and people. But scientists do not believe that.

Explorers have searched far and wide for apemen. They have never found any. Yet there are people who insist that they have seen an apeman hiding in the deepest, darkest woods.

Maybe they're trying to explain things that they really saw but didn't understand.

Maybe they're just making up stories.

Or maybe they really saw a monster.

What do *you* think?